To Kenneth
Love, Carolynn & Wayne
Aug 4, 199

ISBN 0 86163 127 7

Copyright © 1985 Award Publications Limited
Spring House, Spring Place
London NW5, England

Printed in Belgium

NIGHT-TiME
Tales

Written by Hayden McAllister

AWARD PUBLICATIONS – LONDON

Benny the Dancing Bear

Benny the Bear's three favourite things were honey, singing and dancing.
Benny lived in a house at the foot of the hill.

On top of the hill was a well.

Every morning after Benny had eaten his breakfast he would climb to the top of the hill with two buckets and fill them at the well.

The trouble was, Benny liked to sing and dance on the way down. So when he arrived home, half the water had spilt out of his buckets!

When the local carpenter heard about Benny's problem, he made some wooden lids to fit on to the buckets.

Now Benny can sing and dance with his buckets, and he doesn't spill a drop of water. Well perhaps just a little!

Captain Bodger's Friends

Captain Bodger had a boat which he called 'The Seadog'.
He always kept 'The Seadog' shipshape and ready to sail.

Sometimes Captain Bodger would get on his boat and go and visit his friends who lived out at sea.

There was a friendly whale called William who had once towed Captain Bodger back to harbour when 'The Seadog' had broken down.

There were seagulls which liked to land on the cabin of 'The Seadog' and talk to Captain Bodger about the weather.

Captain Bodger also knew a pelican called Pedro. Pedro the Pelican often perched on a post and sang sea songs in a pelican voice. When Captain Bodger heard Pedro sing, he would play along on his foghorn.

Star Attraction

Sam the Seal and Jumbo the Elephant were performing animals in the same circus. They had always been the best of friends. But they had never worked *together*, until one day Jumbo came to watch Sam the Seal playing in the pool.

"I have an idea!" said Jumbo. "Why don't I stand on the edge of the pool and hold a hoop in my trunk…?"

Sam the Seal smiled and clapped his flippers together: "Yes! And I can jump out of the water and through the hoop!"

When the circus master saw them playing together he made Sam and Jumbo's act the star attraction at the circus!

Reading Lamp

Brock the Badger lived in a big gloomy house underneath the ground.

It had always been too dark to read in Brock the Badger's house…until he met his friend Willie the Glow Worm.

Willie was a bright glow worm in more ways than one. And he soon came up with a bright idea to help Brock the Badger read in the dark…

As Brock sat in his armchair with a book in his hand, Willie sat on top of the book and glowed brightly.

Knights of the Round Table

Toby the Tortoise has always been interested in King Arthur and his Knights of the Round Table.

One day Roger the Rabbit and Rob the Red Squirrel came to visit Toby. After having some beans on toast together, Toby told his friends he'd like to play a special game. He called it 'Knights of the Round Tortoise.'

"Sir Roger Rabbit can ride on my back," said Toby.

"And I'll be Sir Rob Red Squirrel," chirped Rob.

The three friends had great fun together. They used dustbin lids for shields. Roger the Rabbit made himself a boxing glove lance. And Toby charged along at twice his usual speed.

The Sunny Lands

Roger Rabbit had a special gift. He could talk to the birds.

Some of the birds used to tell him tales of distant lands where the sun always shone.

Roger Rabbit grew very friendly with these birds, but when autumn came and the leaves began to fall, the birds had to say goodbye.

"We're flying off to distant lands where the sun shines," they chorused. "The winter is *far* too cold for us, so we must go now before it is too late. But we'll see you again next spring. Goodbye Roger!"

Poor Roger was *so* upset! The friendly birds had gone, and they wouldn't be back for such a long time…

Roger Rabbit's family and friends tried to cheer him up. But Roger remained a sad rabbit until Carl the Caterpillar suggested: "Why don't you build yourself a little aeroplane? Then you can fly away to see the sunny lands with the birds next autumn."

Roger was so excited with the idea that he began building his aeroplane the very next day.

When the birds returned the following spring, Roger told them about his aeroplane.

Summer passed, and they all had a wonderful time together.

When autumn came, Roger was ready to fly off with his feathered friends to the sunny lands.

All his family and neighbours came to see him off.

"See you next spring!" they cried, as he took off in his aeroplane and waved goodbye.

Big Grey Wolf

Big Grey Wolf was striding down the road with a big stick in his hand. He looked very cross indeed!

Two birds pecking at some crumbs in the road flew away quickly when they saw him coming. "Big Grey Wolf is in a bad mood," said one. "We'd better warn the other animals to keep away from him."

The two birds flew along the road warning rabbits and frogs and mice as they went. "Watch out!" they cried. "Big Grey Wolf is coming. And he's in a *mean* mood!"

When two red squirrels heard that Big Grey Wolf was coming their way they both hid. One took cover behind a tree and the other hid behind a big red and white toadstool.

When Big Grey Wolf strode past them they heard him muttering to himself.

"I'll show them," he was saying. "I'll show them how to hit that ball!"

"I know where Big Grey Wolf is going," chuckled one of the squirrels.

"He's going to play rounders on the village green with the Bear family."

Bongo and Pablo

Bongo the Bear liked to sit in his armchair with a book in his paws. His teacher was called Pablo, and Pablo was a parrot.

Pablo would perch on the back of Bongo's chair.

When Bongo the Bear saw a word he didn't know he would point to it. Pablo would then tell him what the word meant.

And when Pablo didn't know what the word was, he would fly off and ask his dad, who was a wise old bird.

Thirsty Mouse

Melinda Mouse wanted a drink of orange juice. She went to the supermarket to buy some but the man told her they didn't have any cartons of orange juice for mice.

Luckily, Melinda had a friend called Frank who had an ice cream and soft drinks shop. So Melinda went to see him.

"I'd like some orange juice please Frank," squeaked Melinda. Frank poured Melinda a big glass of orange juice and put a straw in it. Then he put a toy ladder up against the glass.

Melinda climbed up the ladder and had a nice refreshing drink of orange juice through the straw.

Benny's Pigeon

Benny Bear had a pet pigeon called Feathers. Feathers lived in a pigeon house which Benny had built for him.

Feathers was very tame and he liked Benny to tickle the top of his head with an ostrich feather.

Three times a week, Benny Bear carried Feathers out into the country in a special basket.

When they were a long way from home Benny opened the basket and let Feathers fly free. Feathers always soared up into the sky, circled once or twice and raced back towards home.

Before Feathers was out of sight, Benny would be running to the nearest bus stop to catch a bus home too.

If Benny arrived first he would put some peanuts in a bowl for his pet pigeon. Benny knew that it wouldn't be long before Feathers would come gliding out of the sky to eat his favourite meal.

Mrs Green's Garden

Mrs Green lived in a cottage on top of a grassy bank. Behind the cottage were lots of trees, and at the foot of the grassy bank was a garden. There were lots of flowers in Mrs Green's garden.

In the winter Mrs Green would feed the birds and squirrels and the rabbits because she knew that they needed plenty to eat in the cold weather.

One day Mrs Green took a train to see her sister who lived in Manchester. She was going to stay with her sister for a month, and when she returned to her cottage she expected to find her garden full of weeds. But the squirrels and rabbits liked Mrs Green so much that when she was away they did some gardening for her.

Rob the Squirrel and Roger the Rabbit dug out the weeds and watered the flowers.

When Mrs Green came home, the grass on the bank had been nibbled short by the rabbits, and her garden was bright with flowers.

Good Timing!

Oh dear! Millie Mouse had slept in! And she would be late to see her friend Monty Mouse.

They had arranged to meet by a red toadstool in the corner of a big playing field.

Millie combed her whiskers and put on her favourite hat with the red flower and rushed out of her house.

"Oh, if only I could fly!" she squeaked to herself.

As she ran, Millie saw a pink balloon lying in the grass. She stopped for a moment and picked up the string of the balloon...

Just then a gust of wind blew Millie and the balloon high over the field until she landed next to Monty Mouse and the red toadstool!

"Right on time!" gasped Monty in surprise.

Moonlight Millie

Millie Mouse liked to sleep out of doors.

She loved to watch the moon shining in the night sky. She also liked to see the friendly stars twinkling.

One day, when Millie Mouse was out walking, she found an empty box. Millie filled the box with dried grass and herbs and put the box under her favourite daisy.

"This will make a lovely bed," said Millie Mouse. "Tonight I'll sleep here under the stars with my favourite daisy to watch over me."

Water Music

Sam the Rabbit loved Lucy the Rabbit, and Lucy the Rabbit loved Sam.

Lucy lived in a lovely rabbit house in Yellow Sand Cliff. From her bedroom window she could just see the sea.

One day Sam the Rabbit came to visit Lucy. But before knocking on the door Sam decided to sing her a song. He was just about to start his song when Lucy emptied a bucket of water out of her bedroom window. Poor Sam got soaked! But Sam didn't mind. He still loved Lucy and Lucy still loved him.

"Next time I sing," he said. "I'll wear my raincoat!"

Jumping for Joy

Pickle dreamed of being a show jumping champion. The trouble was, Pickle was so tiny and his legs were so small, he really wasn't built to jump big fences.

Pickle would gallop around his little field jumping over daisies and tufts of grass, and pretend he was jumping over big fences.

One summer's day, a butterfly flew over the fence and into the field. "My goodness!" cried Pickle. "How I wish I could sail over that fence as easily as you. You see, I want to be a show jumping champion." "You look like a champion to me," said the butterfly. "So why not try and jump the fence now. I'm sure you can. I'll fly and whisper encouragement in your ear." So Pickle ran and the butterfly flew towards the fence. Together they sailed over. "We'd make a good team," laughed Pickle, jumping for joy.

Sailing in the Sun

Teddy Toad and George Grasshopper were very good friends. But Teddy Toad liked *wet* weather, and George Grasshopper liked *dry* weather.

Naturally George Grasshopper didn't enjoy visiting Teddy Toad's home by the river bank because it was so damp. So Teddy Toad suggested they go boating in a big waterlily leaf.

With the sun shining brightly, George Grasshopper was able to keep nice and dry in the waterlily boat. And to keep himself happy, Teddy Toad kept diving overboard into the water for a swim.

Pilot Bear

Most people keep a car in their garage. But Basil Bear kept a red aeroplane in his garage.

Every summer's day, unless it was raining, Basil Bear would take his red aeroplane up amongst the clouds.

He liked to look down on the houses and the tree-tops and the fields far below.

Sometimes his friends would wave to him as he passed overhead.

One particular friend called Colin Crow would fly up *above* the red aeroplane and then drop down and land on the tail plane.

When Basil wanted to turn right, Colin Crow would put out his right wing. And when Basil wanted to turn left, Colin would put out his left wing.

When Basil wanted to go straight ahead, Colin Crow would just sit still and enjoy the feeling of flying without having to flap his wings!

Billy the Baker

Billy the Rabbit was a Baker. He made different kinds of cakes and bread and carried them around in a basket. He'd shout "Cakes for sale. Five pence each. Buns for sale. Four pence each. Bread for sale – ten pence a loaf!"

Billy made some lovely cakes and he always had lots of customers.

One person who always bought a cake from Billy the Rabbit was Mrs Tipple who lived at the top of a very tall house.

One day Mrs Tipple wasn't feeling very well and so she couldn't come down to buy her usual cake from Billy the Baker. So Mrs Tipple asked a songbird to go down and collect her cake from Billy.

Billy gave the songbird Mrs Tipple's cake and said: "Little songbird, if you come and see me when I've sold all my cakes, you can have all the crumbs you want from the bottom of my basket."

Bob's Flowers

Bob the Bear had an empty honey barrel in his garden. First he painted it, and then he filled it with soil. In the springtime Bob bought some flower seeds and planted them in the soil. When summer came the seedlings grew. So Bob tended the seedlings and watered them when they were thirsty.

Now the old honey barrel is full of colourful flowers. Bob is really pleased, and so are Bob's friends the honey bees, who come every day to visit the flowers.

Mrs McMouse's Tea Party

Mrs McMouse made the best cup of tea in Green Leaf Woods.

Friends would call from near and far just to taste Mrs McMouse's tea. She also made very tasty cakes and pastries.

Mrs McMouse lived in Melon Cottage, not far from Deep Down Well. It was one of the nicest parts of Green Leaf Wood.

One day a stranger came to live on High Top Hill, overlooking Green Leaf Woods. His name was Sir Basil B. Badger.

"He sounds very important I'm sure," said Mrs McMouse. "And we'll have to make him feel welcome in his new home."

So Mrs McMouse and her friends laid on a tea time treat especially for Sir Basil B. Badger.

When Sir Basil B. Badger tasted Mrs McMouse's tea, he said: "Mrs McMouse you make the best tea I've *ever* tasted, and your cakes are delicious too!"

That made everyone feel very happy, and very pleased for Mrs McMouse.